Down a Magic Stream

For Rebecca
Fred Hanson

Ann Hanson

Printed by
PALMER PUBLICATIONS, INC.
Amherst, Wisconsin

Down a Magic Stream

By FRED HANSON
Illustrated by ANN RUSSELL HANSON

BLACK WILLOW PRESS
Fond Du Lac, Wisconsin

Printed in the United States of America for
BLACK WILLOW PRESS
Fond du Lac, Wisconsin

ACKNOWLEDGMENTS

We gratefully acknowledge the help of reading
specialist, Nancy Fetter, and many teachers;
among them, Jane Seibel and Patricia Caspary
who read the manuscript to their classes
to test responses.

A special acknowledgement is due
Megan and Jacob for being models for the
illustrations and to Ashley, the talented
grasshopper guard.

Fred and Ann Hanson
Black Willow Press
Fond du Lac, Wisconsin
April, 1992

For Betsy and Stephie
about a magic time in life.

GLOSSARY

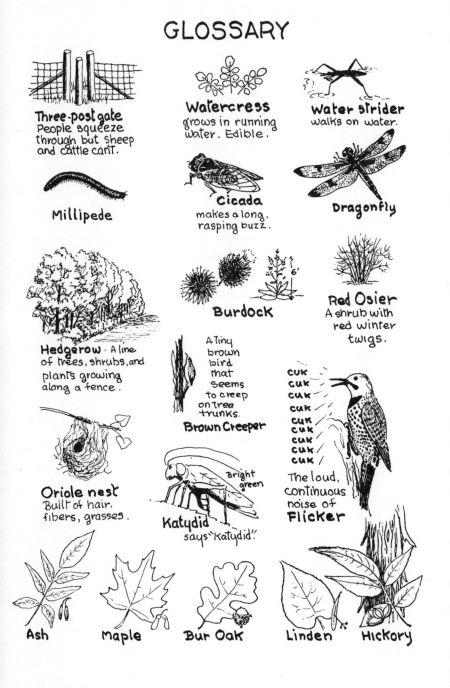

Three-post gate
People squeeze through but sheep and cattle can't.

Watercress
grows in running water. Edible.

Water Strider
walks on water.

Millipede

Cicada
makes a long, rasping buzz.

Dragonfly

Hedgerow - A line of trees, shrubs, and plants growing along a fence.

Burdock

Red Osier
A shrub with red winter twigs.

A tiny brown bird that seems to creep on tree trunks.
Brown Creeper

Oriole nest
Built of hair, fibers, grasses.

Bright green
Katydid
says "Katydid!"

CUK
CUK
CUK
CUK
CUK
CUK
CUK
CUK
CUK

The loud, continuous noise of **Flicker**

Ash **Maple** **Bur Oak** **Linden** **Hickory**

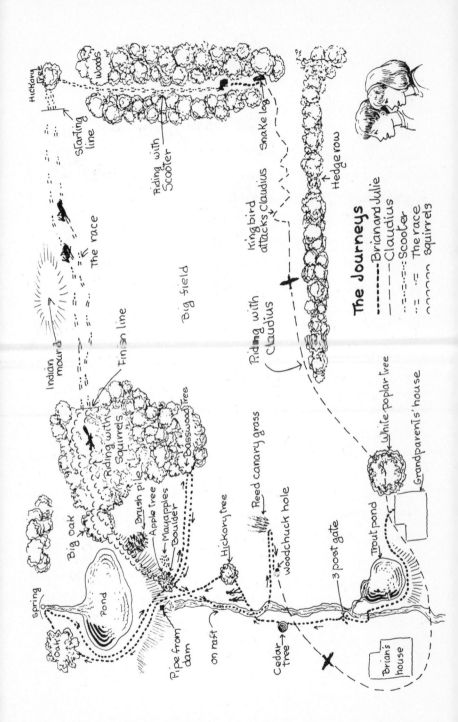

Hickory Tree

Starting line

Woods

Riding with Scooter

Snake log

Kingbird attacks Claudius

Hedgerow

Riding with Claudius

Big field

The race

Indian mound

Finish line

Riding with Squirrels

Basswood Tree

Brush pile

Big Oak

Apple tree

Mayapples

Boulder

Hickory tree

Reed canary grass

Woodchuck hole

White poplar tree

Grandparents' house

Oak

Spring

Pond

Pipe from dam

on raft

Cedar tree

3 post gate

Trout pond

Brian's house

The Journeys

- - - - Brian and Julie
— — — Claudius
·········· Scooter
-··-··- The race
········· Squirrels

CHAPTER I

One of the good things Brian liked about summer vacation was that his cousin Julie and her family came to visit. They stayed right next door at his grandparents farm so there were always lots of picnics and trips together.

This summer they would be there for three weeks and that seemed like a long time, but the days were flying by and all the cousins were trying to make the most of the visit.

Today Brian and Julie decided they'd hike up through the pasture to the spring even though it was pretty hot. This seemed like such an ordinary thing to do, little did they suspect it would turn out to be the day they'd most remember.

Both their mothers were off shopping but they found their grandmother working in her flower garden by the trout pond.

"Grandma," said Brian, "We're going up to the spring. If we aren't back by lunch time, ring the dinner bell for us, okay?" Their grandmother agreed and the two started away.

They slipped through the three post gate to the pasture and followed the valley of the stream up toward the spring.

The water swirled and rippled past the boulders

in the stream bed, glistening in the sun. Across the stream their grandparents' Hereford steers raised their heads to stare at them. A few of them kept on chewing; others just stared, with wisps of grass hanging from their mouths.

The air was still in the valley and the August sun beat down on them. Grasshoppers of many sizes jumped or flew away from them in all directions as they strode through the grass.

They stopped in the shade of a big red cedar that grew near the stream to watch a crowd of black ants towing a dead grasshopper away.

Further up the valley, they crossed the stream balancing on big dark boulders. Then they walked away from the stream out into the middle of the pasture where an old shagbark hickory grew. Here, they stopped again, looking up at it, with its big strips of rough bark curling out from the trunk.

"Look, Julie, up there by that first big branch," said Brian. "There are all kinds of hickory nuts stuffed under that big piece of bark. I'll bet a mouse put them there."

"And look at all the old shells on the ground," added Julie. "They've all got mouse holes gnawed in them. I wonder if the mice live in the tree somewhere."

"If they don't, they've got a place to eat here, anyway," replied Brian.

"If you were as small as a mouse, or you were a

2

They crossed the stream on big black stepping boulders.

butterfly and got caught in the rain, you could get under those pieces of bark and you'd never get wet," said Julie. She pulled one strip of bark out so she could look under it. A big, fat grey spider dropped out.

"Ugh," she exclaimed, letting go of the bark and jumping back. "Is he ever fat! I'll bet he just waits under there for insects to come along."

They watched as the spider traveled slowly back toward the trunk of the tree and started upward again.

"Come on," said Brian, "Let's go."

Out in the sunlight, they turned back toward the stream again. Ahead of them an old apple tree grew below the dam of another pond. Just beyond the old apple, the water from the pond rushed out of a big metal pipe at the base of the dam. It fell to the stream bed with a splashy, gushing sound.

They climbed up over the dam and started around the pond. A short distance above the pond, they came to the spring. Here the water surged out, clear and cold, from between huge shelving rocks.

Both cousins lay down on the flat rocks by the spring, lowering their faces down to the water to drink. When they had finished, they raised their heads, gasping for breath.

Kneeling, they cupped their hands and brought the cool water up to their faces and over their arms again and again.

"Ohhh," exclaimed Julie, "Does that feel good!"

"Mmmm," replied Brian, through a final double handful of water.

A huge bur oak shaded the area about the spring. Julie sat down and leaned back against its trunk. Brian lay full-length on his back, looking up into the branches, his arms flung out in the cool grass. Neither said anything. Above them, a cicada made its first rattling warm-up sounds, greeting the heat of the day; while from the highest branches somewhere in the woods to the east an oven bird gave its harsh "teacher-teacher-teacher" call.

Presently, Julie said, "Let's start back."

They stood up and followed the stream the short distance to the pond. Watching the water, they walked slowly along the shore. If they came too near, water striders skip-jumped away from them on the surface.

Two dragonflies flew past, dipping and darting after each other till they disappeared in the shade across the pond.

The two cousins climbed down the far side of the

Here the water surged out clear and cold.

dam to the iron pipe and the stream below it.

Julie picked up a dead stick and dropped it into the stream. The current caught it and it shot swiftly through between two boulders, over a small waterfall, then turned slowly around in the quiet water below. One end nudged a submerged rock; the current swung the other end clear, and it was in swift water again, zipping around a bend out of sight.

They found other sticks and tossed them into the water, watching them disappear too, betting with each other which one would go the fastest or the furthest.

When they ran out of good floating pieces, they raced downstream to retrieve them. They found a few lodged in beds of watercress; one large one caught between two rocks, and one even stuck on shore. But most of them were still floating free.

After they collected all they could find, Brian said, "I'll stay here. You go back up to the apple tree and put them in again and I'll pick up those that come by."

Again and again they launched their sticks, changing places after each launching. Finally, Brian said, "Let's make a raft out of the best sticks and send stones and other things downstream on it.

"How will we fasten it together?" asked Julie. "You don't have any string, do you?"

"No," replied Brian, "But there's a basswood tree over there by the woods with a lot of young shoots growing up around it. We can pull the bark off where grandpa's steers have eaten the tops or broken them and use the strips of bark to tie the

On top of these, they bound other sticks crosswise.

raft together. Grandpa told me the Indians used to use strips of green basswood bark and willow twigs to tie things together or to make their baskets."

7

The cousins hurried to the woods where they peeled the bark from the damaged shoots, then took it back to the shade of the apple tree.

The two best and largest of their sticks they placed on the ground a few inches apart and parallel to each other. On top of these, they bound other sticks crosswise, one by one to form a platform. When they were finished, they had quite a good-looking raft.

"There," said Brian, "That'll work. I'll go down and wait and you launch it."

He ran downstream and stopped where he could kneel on a big rock and catch the raft as it went by.

"Ready?" called Julie.

"Okay," Brian answered.

Julie launched the raft with a small stone aboard. The raft arrived safely with its cargo, and Brian carried it back upstream. Then they used different stones, and combinations of small and large stones together, to test how much the raft could carry.

Finally, Brian said, "I'm getting tired. Let's rest for awhile under the apple tree and cool off before we go home."

"Okay," Julie answered. "I'm going to leave the raft here where the bank is low. It won't float away, even if it is partly in the water."

The cousins sat down under the apple tree with their backs against a smooth, black boulder. It felt cool against their bodies. They were silent for awhile, then Julie said, "Wouldn't it be fun if we were small enough to ride our raft down the stream?"

"Yeah," replied Brian, "It would really be neat if we could."

There was silence again for a time, with only the splashy whoosh of water coming out of the pipe and the burbling of the stream. They closed their eyes. It was so peaceful they weren't sure they were asleep or awake when a deep, gravelly-kind of voice spoke from behind them. It said,

> "If you don't want to be tall,
> And you'd rather be small,
> Just do what I say,
> And you'll be tiny today."

Both cousins sat up straight. They looked at each other out of the corner of their eyes, then slowly turned their heads to look behind them, but there was no one there. Back of the big boulder was a patch of may apples, and beyond that the grass of the pasture stretched all the way to the woods.

They looked at each other, then Brian asked in a shaky voice, "Where are you?"

Both of them were kneeling on the ground by this time, facing the boulder, and the reply seemed to come right out of the earth in front of them. "I'm right here," the voice said.

"Where?" asked Julie.

"Right by the boulder," came the reply. "Keep watching." The cousins kept their eyes glued to the earth at the boulder's base. Finally, in one spot, it began to move. They stared in fascination, not knowing whether they should run or be brave enough to stay there and see what was going to come out of the ground. Would it be a snake, or a turtle, or a salamander, perhaps? Or would it be a troll, or an earth spirit? Or would it be some horrible earth monster? They held their breaths, their eyes riveted on the ground, ready to scramble up and run.

The earth moved again. Finally a head began to show. When it was above the earth, two bulging eyes blinked open, then a big, fat, earth-colored toad pushed his way up out of the ground. "Hi, you two," he croaked.

"Hi," they both answered with relief.

"So, you want to be small for awhile and have some fun on your raft, eh?" croaked the toad.

Both cousins nodded and the toad continued, "All right, it's very simple. I've done this before. Remember, Julie, the other day when you couldn't find your sister, Kathy? Well, one of my brothers lives under a big rock by the back door to your grandparents' house. He helped her to change to 'smallest', and then she changed back again after awhile. And remember, Brian, after you found her and you asked her where she'd been, she said, 'Oh,

10

I've just been around different places.' The truth of the matter was that she had been, too." The toad gave a gravelly chuckle, then went on, "In fact, she had to scoot under the spruce tree below the trout pond waterfall to keep from being stepped on, one time when you ran past. But don't ever say anything to her about it, or she'll never be able to be 'smallest' again, if she wants to, and neither will you."

"If we want to be 'smallest', what do we have to do?" asked Julie.

"Very simple," replied the toad. "You wait till I go underground again, then you sit down and lean back against the boulder and shut your eyes. Silently, you say, 'I want to be small, smaller, smallest.' You wait a few seconds, then open your

"Hi, you two," he croaked.

eyes and there you are, hardly bigger than a grasshopper."

"And how do we get to be big again," asked Brian.

"When you want to be big again, do the same thing at the same boulder, but instead of what you said in the beginning, you just say, 'I want to be large, larger, largest.' The only thing is you've got to be here at this same boulder or it won't work, okay?"

Both cousins nodded. The toad winked one of his bulging eyes at them and said, "Okay, have a good time." He waddled back to his spot by the boulder and seemed to settle down and flatten out. They watched while he made powerful, pushing movements with his hind legs and worked his body back into the earth. Soon he had disappeared and they couldn't even tell where he had been.

Brian and Julie looked at each other. "Should we?" asked Brian.

"Why not?" replied Julie.

"Okay, I will if you will," Brian said, and both of them leaned back against the boulder.

CHAPTER II

They closed their eyes and said the words, "I want to be small, smaller, smallest" to themselves. When they opened their eyes a few seconds later, they found themselves sitting beside a huge boulder that towered over them. It was at least eight times as tall as they were, for they were both scarcely five inches in height. They stared at each other in wonder. It had really worked! They were "smallest!"

They looked about them with amazement. In the green places the grass was as tall as they were, and when they looked up into the old apple tree, it towered way above them, seeming to disappear into the sky. The leaves appeared to be almost as long as they were and the green apples hanging from their twigs looked like huge muskmelons.

A black ant poked its head out through the grass. Its antennae worked at the air. But this was no common ant. It looked as long as Julie's forearm and stood up on its six legs as tall as her ankles. The cousins shrank back against the boulder. The ant peered about briefly, then ran rapidly in another direction, its huge pincher-like jaws at the ready.

"Boy, that ant was scary," said Julie.

"Yeah," replied Brian. "We'd better get some clubs."

They both hunted about until they found pieces of wood the right size. When they were armed with these, Julie said, "Before we go down the stream on our raft, let's explore the may apples." Brian agreed and they walked around the boulder, carrying their clubs, and headed toward the may apple clump. The may apples no longer looked like plants to them, but instead resembled huge, palm trees. They grew thick as a forest and the ground beneath them was bare, for their great umbrella-like leaves shaded the earth completely. Their trunks were as big around as the children's arms. Their fruits, a pale, cream color, hung like Japanese lanterns, high above.

It was shady and cool beneath the canopy of may apple leaves and they wandered about, enjoying the grove. They found that if they pushed at the fleshy trunks, they could make them sway back and forth. They pushed different plants for awhile and when they tired of this, they started back toward the boulder. Beyond the boulder the grass grew tall and thick, almost all the way to the stream. They pushed their way through it until they reached the bank. But the stream didn't look or sound like a stream to them anymore, but more like a river. The water looked swift and wild as it

It was shady and cool beneath the canopy of may apple leaves.

swept past them and around the big boulders in its path.

They stared at it, and Brian said, "It looks pretty scary. When you're this small, it looks like a really big river. Do you suppose we should take a chance and go down it on our raft anyway?"

"Well," said Julie, "Why don't we try it? We can both swim. If we tip over, we could get out all right," and with that, she picked up one of their discarded sticks to use as a rafting pole, and walked out onto the raft.

Brian pulled the other pole from the raft, and sticking it under the end on shore, heaved upward to help move the raft into the stream. When he felt it beginning to move, he threw his pole aboard and scrambled onto the raft after it. As soon as he was safely on, he snatched up his pole again as the raft moved out into the current.

For quite a distance the stream was swift, but their ride was fairly smooth. The two rafters stuck their poles into the bottom at either side of the downstream end of the raft and nudged it on one side or another to keep it moving in the direction they wanted. They drifted rapidly along between high, grassy banks, and past huge beds of watercress humming with insects. The raft glided over one rocky ripple, then around a bend in the stream, and past a thick bed of watercress. They could now look downstream for a long distance.

The water was no longer smooth, but surged and churned in and out between huge boulders as far as they could see.

"Julie," said Brian, "See those first big boulders? Let's try to steer between them."

"All right," replied Julie, and the two poked and nudged the raft, keeping it in the main flow of the stream. The raft slid closer and closer to the boulders, seeming to pick up speed as it drew nearer to them. The boulders loomed ahead, growing larger by the moment. They and the water surging between them was all the two rafters could see.

"Pull in your pole," yelled Brian, and the raft shot swiftly through, just missing both boulders. They had begun to breathe more easily again when the raft ground against a submerged rock and spun around, tilting dangerously. Both of them were thrown to their hands and knees and they clung to the lashings to keep from being swept overboard. The raft slowly righted itself and slewed around in the other direction.

"Hang on, Brian," screamed Julie. "We're going to hit the next one."

Brian tightened his grip on the lashings of the raft and glanced up to see another boulder right in their path. It towered over them as they bore down on it. He closed his eyes and waited, holding on with all his might. They hit it with a crunching sound. The raft stayed there, locked against it, while the cold waters of the stream poured over them. Then one end of the raft came up and they were swept downstream, turning slowly around and around. They went past boulder after boulder, unable to do anything except hope they wouldn't hit too many more. They ground against one or two and spun away from others. Through it all they clung to the raft, shaking and shivering. Finally

They were past the boulders and drifting in quiet waters.

they were past the boulders and drifting in quiet waters again.

Brian and Julie sat up slowly and looked back. It seemed a miracle that they were unhurt and that the raft had held together. For as far as they could see ahead now, the stream flowed evenly along with scarcely a ripple. They picked up their poles and stood up, beginning to guide the raft once more. The sun was hot, and with the slight breeze blowing, their clothes began to dry.

Their spirits rose and Brian grinned at Julie and began to sing, "Row, row, row your boat," and Julie began the round as Brian started the second line.

After a while they tired of singing, and Julie said, "Isn't this neat?" Brian nodded in agreement.

They were warm again and their clothes were nearly dry. For a long time, then, they drifted happily along, in the warm sunlight, enjoying everything about them.

Ahead of them the stream broadened out and grew shallow, with a long stretch of grassy bank sloping gently down to the water on one side.

"Let's put into shore ahead there and explore," said Brian. Julie nodded.

They poled into the bank, hopped off the raft, and pulled it part way up on shore. Then, with their poles safely stowed under the lashings on the raft, they started up the bank.

To one side of them, in the grass at the edge of the stream, sat a big leopard frog, almost as tall as they. Filled with wonder, they stopped to admire his colors shining in the sun, and to watch his throat bulging out and sliding in with his breathing. As they watched, a fly lit on a blade of grass in front of him. The frog's throat slowed its movement and he seemed to rise up on his toes as if he were going to jump. He stayed that way for a long while without moving. Then, in a motion so fast that they were not sure that they had even seen it, his tongue shot out, hit the fly, and returned it to his mouth. His eyes drew in, he swallowed, and again went back to sitting and breathing normally in the bright sunlight.

"Wow," said Brian.

"He's so pretty," said Julie. "But I could just see him grabbing us with that tongue and trying to swallow us by mistake." Eyes wide, Brian nodded. The two moved up the bank then, pushing between the clumps of grass, glancing back at the huge frog as long as he was in sight.

When they reached the crest of the bank, a dense forest of green grass stretched before them. The sun glinted on blades as broad as their hands. Presently, they came to some larger tufts that arched up over their heads. It was quiet except for the noise they made, pushing through the grass.

Through the stems at the edge, they could see the singers.

As they moved along there seemed to come the sound of singing from somewhere ahead of them. It was faint at first. When the breeze shifted it would almost die out. Then they realized they were hearing the same rowing chant that they had been singing coming down the stream. They tried as hard as they could, but they couldn't understand the words and besides, it didn't sound like human voices. It was a more reedy sound than the voices of people, and more mechanical.

The cousins looked at each other and Brian placed his finger to his lips. Julie nodded and they began to walk slowly forward in the direction of the singing. Suddenly it stopped. They stopped, too, and held their breaths. Had the singers been closer than they thought? Had they seen or heard them coming and stopped because of that? They stood stock-still, breathing as quietly as they could. They strained their ears, listening for any slight sound that they might hear.

After a long while, they both sank down in the shade of a tall clump of grass and continued to listen.

Julie was just going to whisper, "The singing must be over," when the chant began again. It was much nearer this time, and the words sounded clipped and mechanical. They were close enough and it was loud enough so that they could understand a few words. The cousins rose to their feet. Staying in a crouched position, they moved in the direction of the chanting as quickly and quietly as they could. Beside a large clump of grass that arched skyward, they stopped. The sound by this time was so loud that they were sure that the chanters must be right on the other side of the clump. On hands and knees, the two crawled slowly around the tuft of grass until, through the stems at the edge, they could see the singers.

To their surprise, what they saw scattered in a rough circle on the ground were a score or more of big grasshoppers and on blades or stems of grass beyond them were others. These were the singers and in their reedy, rasping voices, they chanted:

"Chew, chew, chew the green,
Chew the juicy green,
Thoroughly, thoroughly, thoroughly, thoroughly,
Like a big machine."

Over and over they sang their chant in two-part harmony. The longer they repeated it, the louder it became, until the noise was almost unbearable. Then, as if on signal, they all stopped singing as quickly as they had begun and walked to the nearest blades of grass and began to eat.

Brian looked at Julie and was going to whisper, "What do you think of that?" when he felt himself grabbed from behind and yanked to his feet. He yelled and heard Julie scream, then realized that both of them were in the grasp of huge grass-

The guards marched the two captives to the rock.

hoppers. These hoppers were standing erect on their jumping legs, holding the cousins' arms with the hooks of their other four legs. One was on either side of them, and a third stood behind each of them, grasping their hair. Standing upright on their jumping legs, their heads were at the children's shoulders. Brian and Julie tried to struggle, but they were helpless. The grasp of the hoppers was vise-like.

"It's no use, little humans," said the largest

grasshopper in his reedy voice, "You can't escape us."

All the other grasshoppers had stopped eating and were gathering around the cousins and their captors. They stood on their jumping legs and waved their front legs and antennae about. There were angry shouts of "Kill them! Tear them apart! Chew them up!" The crowd milled about. The grasshoppers that had captured the children tried to keep between them and the other grasshoppers, but the situation was becoming tense. The guard hoppers were far outnumbered. Would the mob attack the guards, overcome them, and tear the children apart? The grasshoppers waved their legs, their mouth parts working in anger. Brian and Julie were paralyzed with fright. Suddenly, the guard leader started to sing the chewing song. As if by magic, the angry shouts subsided and everyone began chanting the song, over and over. Surrounded by all this noise, Brian and Julie felt almost faint. They wondered what would happen to them next. Again, as if on signal, the chant abruptly stopped and all of the grasshoppers, except the guards, started to eat as if they had simply forgotten about the children.

The guard leader said, "Come on, little humans," and started walking through the grass.

"Where are you taking us?" asked Julie.

"To our queen who lives in a clearing in the reed

canary grass at the edge of the meadow. She'll hear your case and decide what to do with you. Whatever she decides, I don't think it will be a pleasant fate," he added.

They marched along, the children surrounded by the big guard hoppers. Brian glanced behind him and saw that they were being followed by many other grasshoppers of all ages and sizes and shades of green. Word must have spread, for the mob grew larger the further they walked. They finally reached the reed canary grass and followed a well-marked path that led toward the center of the growth. The grass was very tall and grew close together, its stems swaying slowly in the breeze. The blades made a harsh sound when they brushed against each other. In the very center, they came to an opening. There lay a huge flat rock with a smaller round one on top of it. On the round rock sat the queen grasshopper. The guards marched the two captives to the rock where the queen awaited them.

All the grasshoppers had crowded into the opening. They settled themselves on the ground, leaving only an open aisle down the center.

The queen arose and waved her antennae for silence. When there was quiet, she seated herself again, and fixing the two children with a hard stare from her enormous eyes, asked in a raspy and unpleasant tone of voice, "What have we here?" as she continued to glare at them.

The guard leader answered, "These are two little humans that we found spying on us at the feeding ground, your Grace."

"HHhhMMMmmm," said the queen, "And what do you have to say for yourselves?" she asked in her grating voice.

The cousins looked at each other, not knowing which should speak first. Then, as Julie was about to speak, the queen waved her antennae at them and said, impatiently, "Come on, come on! Speak, up, speak up!"

Brian began to tell her their story, how they had gone for a walk, gotten "smallest" with the toad's help, and started down the stream on their raft. By the time this much of the story had been told, they could both see that the queen was becoming thoroughly impatient again. Her eyes shone red and she thrashed her antennae at them.

She silenced Brian with a rasping, "Enough! Enough! We can't sit here all day listening to such drivel. I suppose you're going to tell us that you've never killed a grasshopper or have never cut any of their best eating grass."

"Oh, your Majesty," broke in Julie, "We never have!"

The queen glowered at them and snorted a raspy, "Hummph!" then continued, "No matter. Even if you haven't, I'm sure your relatives have.

Silence from now on!" She turned to the assembled grasshoppers and said, "I will now hear testimony in the small humans' behalf." She waited for what seemed a long time, but there was only a dead silence. No grasshopper spoke up in their defense. "Very well," said the queen, "If there is no favorable testimony, I will now hear testimony against them."

Instantly, a scarred, old grasshopper jumped to his feet, waving his antennae. The queen recognized him. "Your Grace," he said, "Humans kill us. They put hooks through our bodies and throw us into water where fish eat us. When they think we have gotten too numerous, they poison us. I say kill the little humans!" There was a roar of agreement from the crowd. A number of grasshoppers rose on their jumping legs, waving their antennae and front legs, and shouting, "Yes! Yes! Kill them! Kill them!"

Brian and Julie were shaking with fear. Julie thought, Is this really happening to us? She looked at Brian and could see the fear in his eyes too.

There were more shouts of anger from the mob of grasshoppers and the queen waved her antennae until there was silence.

Then she spoke, "Loyal subjects," she said, "This is an unusual opportunity. Most humans are too big for us to do anything to them, but these two are very small and we will have some revenge for a change. All those in favor of the death penalty, say Aye."

There was a raspy "Aye" from the mob gathered in the royal clearing.

"Opposed?" asked the queen, and there was not a sound. "Carried," said the queen. "And now," she continued, "The question is, how shall we kill them?"

Cries of, "Chew them up! Kick them to death! Tear them apart!" burst from the mob of grasshoppers. The queen waved her antennae, holding up her two pairs of front legs as well, until once more there was silence.

When it was quiet, she recognized the grasshopper guard leader, who said, "Your Grace, I have been thinking about this problem ever since we captured these two. Since the death penalty is the unanimous choice, I think I know of a method that will meet with everyone's approval. I suggest that we tie them up with saw grass and put them on the big ant hill by the old hickory tree in the pasture. I'm sure the ants would be more than pleased, and the little humans' deaths would be slow and painful enough to satisfy any among us who thirst for revenge."

The guard leader had scarcely finished talking before cheers and shouts of approval broke out. The queen held up her first pair of legs for silence again. When it was once more quiet, she spoke.

"You have all heard the suggestion from Gerard, the guard. Is there any discussion?"

No voice was raised, and when the queen said, "All in favor," there was again a thunderous "Aye" in response.

Brian and Julie clutched at each other and drew closer together. Julie said, "I can't believe this, Brian! Tell me we're dreaming."

"We're not dreaming, Julie," replied Brian. "They really want to kill us, and I'm scared. What can we do?"

The cousins broke off their whispered conversation when they realized the queen was speaking to them. "I repeat," she said, "Have you anything to say for yourselves before sentence is carried out?"

With tears in their eyes, the children shook their heads, too stunned to think of anything to say.

CHAPTER III

"Very well," continued the queen, "Have you any last request before the sentence we have agreed upon is imposed on you? If you have, you may speak with each other and present a joint request, if you wish. But if you do, be quick about it!"

Brian and Julie drew even nearer to each other so they could whisper without being heard by anyone, and Julie said, "I've got an idea, Brian, and I think it's our only chance. Whenever they sing the chewing song, they drop everything until they're through, and they always sing it at least six times. When I say 'Go', I'll start singing it to the grasshoppers on my side of the clearing and you bring the ones on your side in on the second line."

"And then we'll run for the stream!" broke in Brian.

"Yes," said Julie. "Okay, are you ready, Brian?"

"Ready," replied Brian.

"Go," said Julie, and she turned to the grasshoppers on her side of the clearing and began chanting,

"Chew, chew, chew the green,"

waving her arms all the while. She was scarcely on the second word when they all joined in and as

There they were, facing a big, angry-looking woodchuck.

they began the second line, she heard Brian and
the grasshoppers on his side begin the chant as
well. At that, the two cousins turned and raced
down the open aisle and out of the queen's
chamber. Down the path in the reed canary grass
they flew. When they came to the edge of the
pasture, they dodged between the clumps of grass,
running as fast as they could toward the stream. If
there was any singing going on behind them, they
could no longer hear it. They ran on and on, their
breaths coming in gasps. Finally they came to a
big boulder that they remembered was about halfway to the stream. By now they were sobbing for
breath and nearly exhausted. They leaned against
the boulder, taking in big gulps of air and watching to the rear for any signs of the grasshoppers.

Presently, with fear in his voice, Brian said, "There they are. I saw the first ones hopping this way."

"Come on, then," said Julie. "We've got to run some more. We've just got to reach the stream!" They both turned toward the stream again and ran as fast as they could. They were looking back as they rounded another boulder, so neither of them saw the mound of grey and brown fur they ran into.

Both of them bounced off the owner of the fur who gave a loud "WWUUUuuFFFff" and whirled about to face them.

There they were, facing a big, angry-looking woodchuck who had been sunning himself by the entrance to his burrow.

"Oh, Mr. Woodchuck," they said, "We're sorry to bump into you like that."

"We're running away from the grasshoppers," added Julie.

"They were going to kill us," broke in Brian. "They were going to tie us up in saw grass and put us on an ant hill."

All the while the two were talking, the woodchuck had been blinking his eyes rapidly, trying to wake up. He said nothing and seemed to have a problem understanding what the cousins were talking about. Finally he burst out with, "Nuisance! Grasshoppers are the biggest nuisance there is! Eat all the best grass so there's none for anyone else. You hide in my burrow and I'll stay at the entrance and protect you and we'll fix them, believe me. I'll send goldfinch after the crows. That will fix those grasshoppers right."

As the children hurried toward the entrance to his burrow, they heard the woodchuck call to a goldfinch perched on a bull thistle nearby, busily eating seeds. "Goldie, please go get the crows. Hurry as fast as you can. Tell them there's plenty of hoppers in the meadow." From the burrow the children caught a glimpse of the goldfinch flying away and heard him repeating over and over in rhythm with his dipping flight,

"I'll tell the crows,
Oh yes I will,
Come to the meadow,
And eat your fill."

The two cousins continued down the burrow. It grew darker and they stopped walking until their eyes became used to the dark. A few more steps took them around a bend in the tunnel. They could see light ahead of them and shortly they entered the woodchuck's living chamber, a very comfortable room with a dried grass floor and a big, mound of dry grass at one side. Everything was bathed in a soft light coming from scores of glow-worms trapped in an old glass jar. With a sigh of relief, the cousins sank down on the mound of grass and closed their eyes. They had no idea how long they had been there or even if they might have been asleep when they heard the woodchuck's voice calling to them excitedly, "The crows are here! The crows are here! Come and watch the fun!"

They scrambled up to the mouth of the burrow and crouched down by the side of the woodchuck. He was grunting and chuckling in delight, saying over and over, "Good! That'll fix 'em!"

Scattered over the grass was a huge flock of crows. But what birds they were! They stood much taller than Brian and Julie, and they had big, wicked-looking, black beaks. They were pursuing, with great hops and even short flights, all the grasshoppers that remained in the meadow. While they did this, they carried on a constant string of crow-talking and exclamations. The children could see grasshoppers being caught with lightning-fast pecks of those huge beaks.

Beside them the woodchuck grunted and mumbled his approval. Brian and Julie couldn't believe how quickly the grasshoppers were gobbled up. Soon no more hoppers were to be found, and the crows strutted about, wiping their beaks on the ground and preening themselves. A few of them flew to the highest branches of the old hickory in the meadow. A quarrel broke out among them about who had guard duty the next time there was a feast like this. The squabble got louder and louder until a big, old crow flapped up to a branch near them. It took only a few low, hoarse croaks and caws from him to settle the argument. After a bit, some of the flock on the ground rose into the air and flapped away. Most of the crows in the hickory joined them and a few others slipped away into the woods. There was much calling and cawing between the departing birds and those behind in the meadow even long after all were out of sight of each other.

The woodchuck stirred himself and said, "There, that takes care of that. Now you can be safely on your way. Where was it you said you were going? Can't seem to remember."

"We didn't get a chance to tell you where we were going, everything was happening so fast when we bumped into you," said Julie.

"Oh yes, now I remember," said the woodchuck, "You were running away from the grasshoppers." Mention of the grasshoppers set him off again. "They're a nuisance. Just a downright, diggity-dog nuisance, that's all they are," said he, as he gave an indignant kick at a rock in the burrow mound.

"We were on a raft trip down the stream and we had beached our raft to do some exploring when the grasshoppers caught us," said Brian.

The woodchuck was still fussing and muttering

about grasshoppers and the cousins weren't sure he had heard Brian at all, but he roused himself from his tirade long enough to say, "Down the stream on a raft? That's dangerous! Much too dangerous! I'd never do that! Believe me. Not me! Nosiree! I never go near water if I can help it. Too

"Just climb up and sit one behind the other."

wet! Too wet for me! I like it dry! By the way, I don't even know your names. I'm Homer T. Woodchuck."

"I'm Brian, and this is Julie," said Brian.

"We're cousins," broke in Julie, "And we really want to thank you," she added, but she got no further when Homer interrupted her.

"Cousins, you say? I had a cousin one time. Didn't do anything but sleep. Laziest woodchuck I ever knew. Reminds me, think I'll take another nap myself. All this excitement makes me tired. Goodbye now. Take care," and he turned away and disappeared down his burrow without another word.

There were still a score or more of crows in the meadow swaggering about, occasionally finding a hidden grasshopper and devouring it. A few more left. Then a big, shiny one, eyed them for a moment and swag-tailed over to the woodchuck mound where they were standing.

He cocked his head at them, then bowed and said, "Hi, you two. I'm Claudius Crow. Want to go up for a flight?"

Brian said, "Hi, Claudius. I'm Brian and this is my cousin, Julie." Then he hesitated because his mother had told him never to take rides with strangers.

But Julie broke in with, "Sure, Claudius, we'd like to go up," and Brian nodded eagerly and grinned to himself because, after all, his mother hadn't said anything about rides with strange crows.

"Can you take both of us up at once?" Brian asked.

"Sure, it's no big deal," answered Claudius. "I'm plenty strong. Stronger than any of them," and he poked his beak in the direction of the remaining crows in the pasture.

"Where do we sit?" asked Brian.

"Just climb up and sit one behind the other on my shoulders," answered Claudius. "Slide your legs under my feathers," he continued, "And hold on to a couple, okay?"He crouched down on the ground and Julie climbed on, with Brian taking a seat behind her.

"Ready?" asked Claudius as he stood up. Then, without waiting for a reply, he took a few running steps and leaped into the air. His wings began a powerful flapping, and they were off! It was like being on a roller coaster. Both children held on as tightly as they could. When they could relax enough to look down, the ground was far below them. They were sweeping in a big circle high above the stream and meadow and even above the upper pasture. Their grandparents' steers looked like fat, little, red and white puppies lying in the shade.

Julie leaned forward and yelled, "Claudius, can you circle over both houses and land in the top of the big, white poplar by grandma's?"

Claudius looked back briefly and said, "Sure." He circled over Brian's house and the children could see Kevin, Julie's younger brother, playing in the yard with Brian's younger brother, Larry. They both yelled at the boys, forgetting that they were so small that their voices didn't carry. Neither boy looked up. Then they were sailing over the pond, toward their grandparents' house. Claudius had his wings set and was gliding in for a landing on a branch at the top of the poplar. The children could see their grandmother still busy in one of her gardens and their grandfather mowing

Away they went, Claudius keeping a steady, flapping beat.

a section of lawn. They looked forward and saw the top of the big poplar rushing at them with alarming speed. Claudius flapped his wings hard a few times. The poplar tree slid under them, and

Claudius came to a perch on a top branch.

He folded his wings and then flipped them slightly a few times and said, "Nice view, eh kids?"

"Sure is," agreed Brian.

Julie looked around, then said to Claudius, "Can you fly to the woods on the other side of the big, sliding hill and back to the stream where you picked us up?"

"Sure, easy," was the reply, and away they went, Claudius keeping a steady, flapping beat. The fields and hedge rows slid past them and far away, by the shore of the lake, the houses slowly changed position. They were about halfway to the woods when both children saw a small, grey bird. It was about twice the size of a sparrow, with a white breast and white tips on its tail feathers. From its perch on the top of a tree in the hedge row it rose quickly up at them.

Brian was just going to ask Claudius what the bird was and what it wanted when Claudius said, in a frightened tone of voice, "CAAaawrr, darn it! Just my luck! Here comes a kingbird. CAAaawrr!" he moaned and began to fly as fast as he could toward the woods. The kingbird speeded up too. It took short, powerful strokes with its wings, at the same time making a harsh, rattling sound. When he was above Claudius and the children, he set his wings and swooped down at them. He zoomed past, almost hitting Claudius on the head, while he snapped his beak loudly.

"Aawwrrr," Claudius whimpered and dipped his wings so that he slid from side to side as he dove earthward. The children hung on for dear life, too frightened to say anything. Claudius used the speed of his dive to shoot them skyward again, then he continued to fly as fast as he could for the woods. The kingbird rose above them, his crest up, crying fiercely. He was getting ready for another dive at them when Claudius spoke. "I'm afraid," he quavered. "Hold on the best way you know how. I'm going to dive when he does and side-slip. I hope I can get into the woods. AAWWwwwrr, here he comes," and he broke off into a whimpering cawing.

The woods was straight ahead of them, and as the kingbird began to dive, so did Claudius. The children clamped onto Claudius' feathers, and when he sideslipped the kingbird shot past them, calling harshly. Claudius just righted himself in time to shoot into the woods between the trunks of the trees, seeming to pick up speed as he flew. He finally slowed his flight and came to a perch on a low branch of an old maple tree in the center of the woods. It was only then that the children could see how frightened he really was. He was shaking with fear. He lowered himself down and said, "Please climb down onto this limb. That was a close call, believe me. If that kingbird had hit us, we might not have come out of it alive," and he shook his head slowly.

The cousins clambered down onto the limb, and Brian said, "Claudius, why are you afraid of kingbirds? You're much bigger than they are."

Claudius answered, talking very fast, "It's because kingbirds have always chased crows. They can fly faster than we can and they threaten to do terrible things to us. You probably couldn't understand what he was saying, but he said," and Claudius was nearly crying with fear, "He said we were too near his nest and if he caught me he'd crush my skull between his talons and tear off my beak."

"But Claudius," said Julie, "He doesn't have any talons, and he's only a quarter as big as you are. He couldn't do that."

"I don't care," blubbered Claudius, "You just don't know what it's like being a crow and having kingbirds chase you." Then abruptly, he said, "You'll just have to stay here. I can't carry you anymore. I'm going to have to sneak back to the flock somehow, where I'll be safe. I should never have let you talk me into taking you for a flight in the first place." Claudius crouched down on the limb, ready to take off.

"But Claudius, wait!" cried Brian. "How will we get down to the ground and get back to our raft? The raft must be a mile away from here, and this branch is at least six feet up in the air."

"Oh, someone will come along and help you," replied Claudius. "Besides," he called as he flapped away, "You should have thought of that before you went for a flight," and his voice faded away.

The two children looked at each other. Then they looked about them. All they could see were dark trunks of trees and a heavy canopy of leaves, far, far above. It was very quiet in the woods.

"Julie," said Brian, "How are we ever going to get down off this limb? We can't jump down and we can't climb down."

"I don't know, Brian," was Julie's reply, and she looked forlorn. "It was so much fun to go for a flight, and then to have it end up this way." Her voice trailed off and she stopped talking.

CHAPTER IV

The cousins sat quietly. The silence in the woods seemed to press on them. They were deep in their own thoughts and none of them were happy ones. It was quiet, so quiet! Suddenly, Brian thought he heard the sound of feet above him; a lot of tiny footsteps. He looked at Julie to see if she was hearing them too. He found Julie staring at him, her eyes wide. Then both children slowly raised their heads. They looked up the trunk of the tree where the tiny footsteps seemed to be coming from. Both saw the source at the same time, and they started with fear. Coming down the trunk toward them was a huge, fat, grey spider, its eight eyes fixed on them.

When it saw that it had been discovered, it called out to them in a heavy European accent, "Dahlinks! Don't be afraid. I vill not hurt you. Undt don't be afraid uff my speaking mit an agcent. I came to this country in the fake flowers on a voman's hat ven I vass chust a small girl spider and, zorry to zay, I haff still an agcent. I am Cassandra Spider, coming to help you. I am hearing you vanting a vay down from that limb, and no vone! no vone! can make a rope for you as guut as I can. You vant to get down? I help you," she said as she reached the limb.

The two children had relaxed by this time and Julie said, "Oh, Cassandra, we're Julie and Brian, and we're so glad to see you. It would be wonderful if you could help us."

When she came to them on the limb, her huge, round body slid easily past them.

She picked a likely spot a short distance beyond at the end of a stub. Here, placing the spinerettes at the end of her abdomen together, she released a strand of sticky substance which she anchored on the stub.

"It vill be a pleasure to help you. Zee I show you," she said.

Slowly, then, she lowered herself head first into space. Her two hind legs on the quickly drying strand controlled the speed with which her body dropped.

When she reached an old log lying on the ground, she fastened the other end of the strand there and rested briefly. Then, as the cousins watched in fascination, she climbed slowly upward spinning another strand onto the first.

"Vonce more," she said when she reached the stub, and repeated the down and up process adding yet another strand both ways.

Back up at the stub again Cassandra walked off onto the limb and said cheerily, "There Dahlinks, now you can zlide all the vay down in zafety."

Slowly, then, she lowered herself headfirst into space.

"Oh, Cassandra, how can we ever thank you enough?" cried Julie, and Brian said, "Cassandra, you've just done the impossible for us. Thank you! Thank you!"

Cassandra turned her eight eyes downward and said modestly, "Oh, Dahlinks, it vass notting," but the two children could see how pleased she was.

One at a time they grasped the lifeline Cassandra had spun for them. Brian went first, wrapping his right leg around it so the strand finished acrosss his right instep, the down part extending from the inside of the foot. Then, placing his left foot over the strand on his right instep, he began sliding down. Foot pressure kept him from going too fast and he hand-walked down the strand, letting it slide throught his feet.

When Julie, too was safely down, they both looked up and waved goodbye to Cassandra. They looked about them in all directions. Surrounded by the huge forest trees, they were very aware of how small they were.

They were standing on an old log that lay beside a path. Stubs of former branches stuck out at all angles from it.

"Too high to jump off this end," said Brian. "Let's go down to the other end. Maybe we can jump or climb down there."

As they were moving around the last big stub near the large end of the log, they saw a slight movement in a patch of sunlight ahead of them. They stopped by the stub to watch.

Slowly a dark green and yellow head rose up over the end of the log. While the cousins stared in horror, a few inches of legless body slithered into view. The eyes of the monster glared about, unblinking, and from its mouth its forked tongue darted again and again.

The children ducked behind the stub and watched, their hearts hammering. The horror of their position grew in their minds as the body of a grass snake fully five times their length slid into view.

Frantic with fear, the cousins turned and raced back to the small end of the log. What could they do? They looked wildly about. There was no way to escape. The log was held up in the air by its branches, and to jump from it might mean their death. But an even more horrible death was at their rear, sliding silently toward them.

The snake kept up its measured advance, along the top of the log, its tongue flicking out at them. It had passed the first big stub and was still advancing. Julie and Brian stared at it wild eyed, the first tremblings of fear beginning to shake their bodies.

Suddenly a huge bird, almost as large as Claudius, flashed downward before them. It hit the log a glancing blow and swept the snake off and down onto the ground of the path. There it spread its wings wide over its prey and tore at the snake with its beak. Its long barred tail fanned out and Brian and Julie caught only glimpses of the snake's body writhing beneath the bird.

"Julie," whispered Brian, "That's a hawk."

The two children watched wide-eyed as the bird tore at the snake, shaking it until it no longer moved. Then it folded its wings and crouched, glaring about it for a time with its fierce, wild eyes.

Grasping the body of the snake, it sprang into the air and flapped swiftly away. Up through the trunks of the trees it flew, the limp body of its prey dangling below it.

Brian and Julie stared at each other, scarcely able to believe what they'd seen. Finally Brian said, "Wow, can you believe that happened? Let's go to the other end of the log, quick while we've got a chance, before something else happens."

When they came to the area where the snake had been, they both shivered a little, and the back of their necks prickled in sudden fear.

Climbing down at the large end of the log was easy and they both walked out onto the path.

"Which way do you think we should go?" asked Brian.

"Probably up the path," replied Julie. "That's the direction that dumb Claudius went."

The path led steadily upward and they hurried along. Even though they walked as fast as they could, they were so small it seemed to take forever to get anywhere. Gigantic trees towered about them on either side of the path, and it seemed to take forever just to walk past the trunk of one.

In low, damp places in the path, they saw raccoon tracks half as long as they were tall and in another place there were tracks of a big deer.

"We'll have to watch out for big animals," panted Julie. "They could squash us flat if they stepped on us."

"Yeah," Brian replied shortly.

They had stopped for a rest and were about to start on once more when they heard something on the trail behind them. Quickly they ran off the trail and hid in a clump of wood violets.

Ta-thump, ta-thump, ta-thump, ta-thump, they heard; drawing nearer with every sound.

What could it be? What could make that kind of a noise? Ta-thump, tathump, ta-thump, the strange sound kept on louder and louder. From their hiding place, both cousins caught a glimpse of brown fur, and then a rabbit came hopping into view.

"Mr. Rabbit," Julie called, "We need help."

The rabbit stopped and froze in that position. He peered carefully in the direction of Julie's voice. His ears looked like huge, brown funnels that swept back and forth, searching for the slightest sound. The two children stepped out into view and the rabbit stared at them. His mouth dropped open and his eyes grew bigger and bigger. He looked frightened.

Brian said, "Mr. Rabbit, please don't run away. I'm Brian, and this is my cousin Julie, and we need help to get back to the old apple tree below the dam in the stream valley."

"I won't run away," said the rabbit. "I was just so surprised to see any humans as small as you two."

"Shall we tell you how we got to be small and ended up here?" asked Julie. She was about to start in when she noticed the rabbit was beginning to fidget, so she asked, "Are you in a hurry?"

"Well, yes," replied the rabbit. "I really am. You see, I'm on my way to the red osier races. Hop on my back," he broke in, "I'm going the way you want to go, so I'll take you along and you can tell me your story."

When the children were safely seated, he continued to talk as they moved along the path. "The red osier races are held in the lane that begins at the top of this woods. The final race is being run today. The winner will be crowned fastest rabbit in the township and have his choice of territory. I'm pretty late and I want to get a good seat on the old Indian mound at the high point in the lane. Most of all," he continued, "I just don't want to miss this final race. Lop Ear Louie is running against Brush Pile Ben. I'm sorry," he continued, "I didn't introduce myself, but I'm so excited about the race that I forgot. My name is Delmar Rabbit. All my friends call me 'Scooter', and you can too. Okay, now tell me how you happened to be here, and most of all,

Bobbing up and down on Scooter's back with every hop.

how you happen to be so tiny. I never saw humans so small."

So, as he hopped briskly along, the two children told Scooter the whole story of their adventures so far. When they had finished, he said, "That's an amazing story. Simply amazing! I don't know whether to believe all you've told me or not. I know I've never heard anything like it before."

"It's the truth, Scooter," both children said. They moved along in silence, then, for quite a distance, bobbing up and down on Scooter's back with every hop. They could see that it was getting lighter ahead of them and that they were coming to the edge of the woods.

"How would we get back to the old apple tree from the lane where the races are held?" asked Brian.

"Easy as pie," replied Scooter. "You'd follow the lane where the race is run till you come to the finish, which is by the edge of another woods. Then you go through that woods, and on the other side is the meadow with the stream running through it."

"But that's an awful long way to go," said Julie.

"Well, you'll just have to leap over that problem when you come to it," replied Scooter.

They reached the edge of the woods and were crossing a narrow field. Scooter continued talking. "See that big hickory tree up ahead?" he asked. "Well, that's the start of the race, and the course follows that lane a good quarter of a mile to the woods at the other end." They were nearing the hickory now. There were scores of rabbits of all ages and sizes, hopping or sitting about. Two big, old rabbits were trying to look important. They wore acorn cap badges labeled "official" fastened by a burdock to one front leg. There were two other big, long-legged rabbits wearing cut down oriole nest saddles on their backs waiting at the starting line.

"Those two with the saddles on are Lop Ear and Brush Pile," said Scooter. He whistled quietly and said, "Look at the legs on them, will you?"

Both cousins stared at them and thought that they had never seen any rabbits with such long powerful-looking legs. Finally, Julie said, "Lop Ear Louie really has a bent ear, doesn't he?"

Scooter said, "Oh, yes. Years ago when he was just a youngster he ran into a low fence wire with his ears up, going full tilt. Both ears came out bent. One straightened out, but the other never did."

"Who's going to ride them?" asked Brian.

"A couple of katydids," replied Scooter, "But they don't seem to be here yet."

"If they don't show up by the time of the race, maybe we could ride in their places!" said Brian.

"That would be one way of getting nearer to the old apple tree," chimed in Julie. "Do you think you could talk to the officials for us?"

"Sure, wouldn't do any harm," replied Scooter, and he hopped up to the officials. Brian and Julie dismounted and stood by his side. The officials looked worried, and Scooter came right to the point.

"Have the riders showed up yet?" he asked.

Both officials shook their heads, and one said, "The brown creeper said he heard them arguing about something when he went by the thicket where they live. One was saying katy did and one was saying katy didn't, so I suppose they won't show up till they've settled that dispute. That may be a long while."

"These two children need to get back to the old apple tree below the dam in the stream valley. If the katydids don't show up, how about letting them ride instead?" asked Scooter.

The two officials stared at the children and then looked at each other. "Let us talk it over," one official said. They turned and hopped a short distance away to where Lop Ear and Brush Pile were waiting.

The two cousins watched as the four rabbits talked. They glanced over at Brian and Julie every once in awhile and then up at the sun. Lop Ear and Brush Pile kept shaking their heads, and one time Brush Pile kicked at the ground. The children's hearts sank, for they could see that the two racers were objecting to the proposal. The two officials talked to them for a long time. All the rabbits gathered to see the race and all of the squirrels and birds in the trees stirred impatiently. Finally both Lop Ear and Brush Pile nodded in agreement. The two officials turned and beckoned, and when the children ran over to where the four of them were standing, one official began to explain the race to them.

"The two runners have agreed to the switch in riders in order to be sure that the race takes place," began the official.

Scooter hopped past and broke in hurriedly, speaking to the children, "Pardon me, but I'm going to the Indian mound at the halfway mark. Good luck to both of you!"

"Oh, Scooter, thank you! Thank you!" they both replied.

He waved and hopped away, and the rabbit official that had been talking cleared his throat and continued, "A short distance away from the starting line the course divides into two, and sometimes three, pathways. The runners may choose any path they wish. There are also stumps and bushes to dodge along the way. Near the end of the course, all paths join into one and continue as one till the finish line is crossed at the edge of the woods. Two hummingbirds will be hovering in the air, holding a single spider strand with dandelion seed parachutes fastened to it at the finish. The first runner to break the strand wins. There is a cardinal in the ash tree at the halfway mark that will whistle the 'all ready' signal, and a flicker at the finish will call the 'cuks'. Minerva Millipede will be the official 'cuk' counter. She will use her legs to count the number of 'cuks' it takes the winner to run the course. There will be a practice whistle from the cardinal and a couple of practice 'cuks' first, to be sure that the sound is carrying properly. Lop Ear is bigger than Brush Pile; therefore, Brian will ride him, since he is bigger than Julie. Are the rules clear?"

Both runners nodded. Both riders mounted their steeds. They found that there were holes in the bottom of the oriole nests for their legs to go through. Thick strands of the nest went around the rabbits' necks and around their ribs, back of their shoulders. The nest itself supported the riders well up their backs, and there were even handholds for them to grasp.

When they were safely in the saddles, both Lop Ear and Brush Pile looked over their shoulders and grinned at them. "Just hold on tight, Brian. I'll do the rest," said Lop Ear.

Brush Pile said simply, "Don't fall off, Julie."

The two runners approached the starting mark and waited.

Both official starters stood tall on their hind legs, waving their ears back and forth. There was silence for a moment, then from his perch in the ash tree, the cardinal whistled. From the distant woods, a second later, came the flicker's ringing practice call, "Cuk-cuk-cuk-cuk-cuk." Then there was silence again. The officials both stood up and ear-waved once more. The cardinal whistled. Both runners toed the line, tensed for the start. Their riders bent low over the backs of their mounts, holding on as tightly as they could. At the flicker's first "Cuk," Lop Ear and Brush Pile were away like the wind, bounding side by side down the course.

Riding Scooter had given the cousins some idea what it was like to ride a rabbit. But this was different! This was a race, and they were riding the fastest rabbits in the township. They were unprepared for the blinding speed, the continuous motion, and the lightning-quick changes of direction. Stumps and bushes loomed up before them, and with a quick change of direction, they flashed past and were gone before either of them even had time to gasp with fright. The wind roared in their ears. Tears blurred their eyes, and all the while there was the bounding motion of their mounts and the need to hang on for dear life to keep from falling off. They were only dimly aware of the cries and calls of bird and animal spectators along the way. Then they were in the final, straight stretch of path at the end of the race, with Lop Ear and Brush Pile running neck-and-neck. There was a final roar of sound from the spectators at the finish. They crossed the line and shot into the dim coolness of the woods.

There Lop Ear and Brush Pile came to a stop and turned to hop slowly back to the finish line. It was only then that Brian and Julie saw how many birds and animals had gathered to watch the race. The children dismounted. They found that Brush Pile had won the race by half a leap in 184 'cuks', a new record!

Both the riders thanked Brush Pile and Lop Ear

for carrying them, and they congratulated Brush Pile on his win. They were feeling a little shaky after the race and were looking for a place to sit down, when Scooter appeared from somewhere and said, "I think I've found a ride for you to the stream." He led them to where two fox squirrels were sitting at the base of a big red oak tree eatting a mushroom.

To Brian and Julie, he said, "These are Herbert and Francis Fox Squirrel," and to the two squirrels, he completed the introduction, saying, "These are the two small children, Brian and Julie, that I told you about. They're the ones that need a ride to the old apple tree by the stream." Everyone murmured hello, and there was a touching of paws to hands.

Then, turning to Brian and Julie, Scooter said, "I don't want you two to think I've run out on you. I could have taken you to the old apple tree too, but I promised my wife, before I left for the race, that I'd start back in time to gather some clover for supper, so I really must be getting on."

"Ahh, Scooter," said Brian, "That's all right. You helped us so much anyway."

"Without your help, we'd never be this far," added Julie.

"Well," Scooter replied, with a pleased look on his face, "I'm glad you feel that way. And now," he continued, "I'm off to that clover patch." He waved

The branches were so small the riders didn't know how they could still balance on them.

a quick goodbye and hopped briskly away.

The children turned back to the two squirrels and Herbert spoke up. "We were going to go and check the apples on the old apple tree below the pond today anyway, and you're more than welcome to a ride if you want it. Climb on."

So the children climbed onto the backs of the squirrels and the four of them started out. They had gone only a short distance on the ground when the squirrels started up a big oak tree. "We like to travel in the trees if we can," Francis said. "It's safer that way."

"We're going to have to make some leaps," Herbert added, "But don't be frightened. They may seem scary because the branches sway up and down, but they really aren't dangerous at all. We're going to travel through the woods to the old white oak by the dam and then run along the dam to the brush pile, and from there to the apple tree. This may sound like a pretty roundabout way to go, but it's safer for us than to go straight across the meadow to the apple tree. Hope you don't mind."

"No, I don't mind," said Julie.

"Neither do I, as long as we get there," agreed Brian.

"Okay," said Herbert, "Here we go." Herbert and Francis climbed about halfway up the old oak tree, with Brian and Julie holding on as tightly as they could. They came to a big limb that extended almost straight out from the trunk of the tree. The two squirrels ran nimbly out on it until the branches were so small the riders didn't know how they could still balance on them. Here they launched themselves through the air at the limb of an ash tree a distance away. Both Brian and Julie gasped and shut their eyes, but the next thing they knew when they opened them again, they were safe on a big branch of the ash tree. They moved from the ash to a hickory branch with only a short leap. The riders kept their eyes open when this happened, although it made them gasp when they looked down.

Their journey through the woods had many thrilling moments, but after the first, big leap, neither of them ever shut their eyes again. Toward the end, they neared the old white oak at the south end of the dam. The children still clung tightly to Herbert and Francis and they tensed at every leap, but they were beginning to enjoy the ride. When they reached the oak tree, the two squirrels climbed down the trunk. As soon as they were on the ground, they bounded along the top of the dam till they came to the brush pile. They climbed to the top of the pile and peered about for a few seconds, then dashed to the ground and down to the old apple tree. There they stopped and the two riders slid off their backs and thanked them over and over for bringing them safely back to their big, black boulder. For their part, Herbert and Francis scarcely seemed to notice the thanks, but quickly climbed up the apple tree and began to examine the fruit.

Brian and Julie pushed their way through the tall grass to the boulder and sat down with their backs against it. "Ready?" asked Julie.

"Ready," answered Brian.

The cousins both shut their eyes and repeated to themselves the words, "I want to be large, larger, largest." They were doing the hardest part, keeping their eyes shut for a few seconds, when the dinner bell at their grandparents' house began to ring.

Both children opened their eyes. There they were, sitting under the apple tree with their backs against the boulder, and they were normal size again!

They looked at each other and grinned, then scrambled out into the open.

When the bell stopped ringing, they each took a deep breath and called a long, "COMING," as loudly as they could.

A quick glance at the stream bank, where their raft had been, showed it to be missing. Both children looked for it on the way downstream and at the shallow where they'd beached it, but there was no sign of it. They knelt down, looking more closely, and Brian said, "That's really strange."

"It sure is," Julie agreed. "But remember, Brian," she continued, "We can't talk about this or tell anyone about any of it, even if it was just a dream, or we won't be able to do it again if we ever want to."

Brian nodded and said, "It won't be hard not to say anything, because no one would believe us anyway." They turned away and hurried down the stream.

When they came to the rail fence that led to the

three post pasture gate, they stopped to watch a squirrel sitting on the top rail. It stayed there only a second more, then scampered along the fence until it came to the big cottonwood. Up the trunk it went. Up and up to a big limb that thrust out toward a neighboring black willow. Out on the limb; out, out, until the branches were so small they waved up and down. There it launched itself at the willow, clutching a small branch that bent way down, then up again. Without a pause it ran nimbly on. Both cousins glanced at each other, and a quick shiver ran up their spines. They slipped sideways through the three post gate and Brian started up the path to his house.

"Come on down this afternoon and we'll go swimming, okay?" Julie called after him.

From half way up the hill Brian turned his head and answered, "Okay."